EPISODES

Mohamed M. Yousif

authorHOUSE®

AuthorHouse™
1663 Liberty Drive
Bloomington, IN 47403
www.authorhouse.com
Phone: 1-800-839-8640

Published by AuthorHouse   04/25/2012

ISBN: 978-1-4685-7797-6 (sc)
ISBN: 978-1-4685-7798-3 (e)

Library of Congress Control Number: (pending)

For Yingqiu

Part 1

Swiftly our pleasures glide away,
Our hearts recall the distant day
With many sighs;
The mountains that are speeding fast
We heed not, but the past,—the past,—
More highly prize.

Onward its course the present keeps,
Onward the constant current keeps,
Till life is done;
And, did we judge of time aright,
The past and future in their flight,
Would be as one.

De Manrique
Longfellow

schade dass die Natur nur einen Mensch aus dir schuf,
Denn zum würdigen Mann war und zum Schelmen der
Stoff.
Wir sind gewohnt dass die Menschen verhöhnen was
sie nicht verstehen.

Goethe

One morning I was relaxing on a comfy chair spreading my legs on another chair trying to read but the letters swam before my eyes. Then I switched on to music and the melody of Beethoven crept all over and through my whole body feeding peace and tranquillity to my system. Darwin said about music '*that of producing and appreciating it existed among the human race long before the power of speech was arrived at.*' Perhaps that is why we are so subtly influenced by it. I relaxed and let my dream carry me on. I was often entertained the idea of completing a writing which had tempted me for a long time. The writing of reminiscences through a span of almost thirty years of employment at an organisation reflecting both bitter and sweet experiences were always in my mind. Such reminiscences would have led me through a world of contradictory personalities reflecting the nature of humans endeavour to reach their goals by whatever means they could. Reminiscences popped into my mind like a film rolling back. I set myself to pursue such recollections by all means and to collect the pits and pieces I wrote so far and resume forming the final shape. I fancied I could circumnavigate the world and visit such places like China where I would stroll along Tiananmen Square with *Yingqiu* reminiscing our days in Europe and visiting the exotic places in Peking, as once we promised to visit. I would stroll along the great Wall and recall the history of such tremendous labour. It is said that '*The Wall is the only man-made object on earth which would be visible from the moon.*' I would Continue the journey through the east to the mystic land of Nepal where Siddhartha, the founder of Buddhism and spiritual teacher; was in search of enlightenment and Nirvana which is the perfect peace of the state of mind that is free from desire, anger, distress and other afflicting states. Perhaps I would join Hermann Hesse's imaginary Journey to the East with his League of prominent personalities from different walks of life and who contributed a wealth of knowledge in the fields of music and sciences to humanity through history. Hesse narrated the tale of the events of the journey in his book 'journey to the east' though a great deal of this Journey will remain inconceivable and incomprehensible. But one should continually attempt the seemingly impossible in order to achieve his goal. As Siddhartha, from the east, said:

'*Words do not express thoughts very well; everything immediately becomes a little different, a little distorted, a little foolish. And yet it also pleases me and seems right that what is of value and wisdom to one man seems nonsense to another.*'

Or as one member of the League, put it as follows:

'He who travels far will often see things
Far removed from what he believed was the Truth.
When he talks about it in the field at home,
He is often accused of lying,
For the obdurate people will not believe
What they do not see and distinctly feel.
Inexperience, I believe,
Will give little credence to my song'

Pursuing my dream; I would continue to navigate to the other side of the hemisphere and visit Brazil at the time of Rio de Janeiro Carnival, the public celebration and the fantastic parade. I would venture through Latin America and explore all places such as the Aztec Pyramids; and whatever remained of the Inca and the Maya civilization. Then I would imagine myself on an island in the Pacific to observe the vast calmness of the Ocean deep blue colour and at sunset turned to an infinite set of colours, the water below crystal clear that you observed the coral with fantastic colours and the fish swimming peacefully like butterflies. The vista would look like a magic garden. How wonderful to be away from the hustle and the constant striving in the town with its dark high gloomy buildings and endless traffic of vehicles emitting poisonous gas. An endless list of places came to my mind. Nothing on our planet is more disgusting, more despicable than borders. Borders between countries are hindrance to freedom of movement. In my dream I thought of devising a system of navigation designated by three letters SNS which stands for Spiritual Navigation System which could take you about diffusing through 'map borders', I call them 'map borders' as they exist only on maps. However the use of SNS, would rather be limited in our present time, but no doubt will develop further to be the overwhelming sprit of humans and thus peace will spread its wings all over. No distinction between races, regions and countries would be recognizable; as equality would be dominant and humans would live in peace and harmony. While I was thus carried away by my mind navigating a dream, the cell phone rang interrupting the Majestic symphony of Beethoven and my thoughts. Reluctantly I opened the line and his voice came through 'I have just arrived a couple of hours ago and full of news to tell you . . . if you have time we can we meet in the evening.' he said. 'Hey welcome back . . . sure we can meet . . . maybe at Havelka about seven today in the evening if it suits you' I said. 'At Havelka Great that is fine till then bye'; he responded and the line went dead. I went back to Beethoven and relaxed through his melody and continued my dream. God knows how often I had regretted that I had not part of the time I needed to do some of the things I wanted. I had often entertained my desire with the prospect of just a couple of day's complete idleness, doing nothing but through this idleness I very often travelled through my life backwards and battled a useless fight which was invincible. I retreated to myself, though rarely, for a couple of days as if being not part of this planet . . . totally absorbed within. Time, because it is beyond recall, is the most valuable precious span in one's life and to misuse or waste it; is the most unwise in which man can yield to.

Part 2

Bowed to the earth with bitter woe,
Or laughing at some rare show,
We flutter idly to and fro.

Man's little Day in haste we spend,
And, from its merry noontide, send
No glance to meet the silent end.

Is all our life, then, but a dream
Seen faintly in the golden gleam
Athwart Time's dark, resistless stream?

Lewis Carroll

It was past 16 O'clock and the mild sun rays streaming through the window curtains. I opened the window and a chilly breath flew in. I prepared myself to go down town. The weather was rather pleasant for the mid of May. Happily, it was not rainy and the sun was struggling through thick clouds with its rays penetrating, giving occasional gleams of silvery sunshine. It took me a while to decide what to put on to suit the unpredictable weather. I was hesitant to carry an umbrella or not; then I decided not to, since I would for sure fail to remember where I left. At the underground station, down the escalator I proceeded to the train platform heading to the city centre. The train stopping at a station was laying a string of people like a hatch of identical like insects, a similar hatch boarding the train, and move to the next station to deposit yet another hatch. On the train you observed all sorts of people from all over the world, north to south reflecting their inherited behaviours, a dark skinned fellow chatting on his phone with a very loud voice in unfamiliar language disturbing the old Viennese ladies expressing their discuss with the turn of their heads and murmuring their protest to this strange behaviour. Viennese commuters usually kept very quiet through their journey though some of the younger generation were a bit noisy disturbing the usual serene atmosphere. A lady carrying her little dog in a bag, with his head protruding out of the bag, looking about with his tiny eyes. Most of the young had their MP3 plugged to their ears and swinging to the sound of music. One could hardly hear German spoken; rather, all sorts of eastern European tongues were dominant among the passengers. Women holding their bags tied in their laps or under their arms lest pinched from them, a phenomena observed in the city commuters lately. I left the train at the city centre. It was six O'clock in the evening . . . so I had an hour to stroll through the city centre prior to my appointment. Many tourists were crowding Stephansplatz and in front of the famous St. Stephan's Cathedral. A group of vegetarian campaigner, set in the middle of the square, were distributing leaflets and showing films of brutal slaughter of animals for feeding humans and providing fashionable dresses from the skin of those little animals which were stripped of their skin while still a life and the cattle were killed by a blow between the eyes with a sledgehammer. Their films reflected the barbarism with which the people were killing, skinning alive and torturing the poor animals was indescribable. On the occasion of some coming event of a football match in a

European country, stray dogs and cats were gruesomely murdered, to keep the streets cleaned. But on the other hand human are treating one another the same way torturing and killing and horrifying pictures of torture in the prisons was beyond any imagination. Throughout the human history for instance; invaders were always brutal, they either invade to take something by force or wipe out the indigenous population to replace them. I lingered beside the screen reflecting those brutal killing and I recalled a passage from Bruce Chatwin book *'The Songlines'* where he quoted professor Raymond Dart concluding:

"The blood-bespattered, slaughter-gutted archives of human history, from the earliest Egyptian or Sumerian records to the most recent atrocities of the second world war, accord with early universal cannibalism, with animal and human sacrificial practices

or their substitutes in formalized religion and world-wide scalping, head hunting, body multilating and necrophilic practices in proclaiming this common bloodlust differentiator, this predaceous habit, this mark of Cain that separates man dietetically from his anthropoidal relatives and allies him rather with the deadliest carnivore."

Animals are used for laboratory experiments for research purposes also; in this case we consider two contradictory propositions: *'firstly that the infliction of pain on animals is a right of man, needing no justification; secondly that it is in no case justifiable'.* The later is assumed by those who advocate the total suppression of vivisection. The middle ground between the above two points as suggested by Mr. Dodgson (pen name: Lewis Carroll) in his article *"popular fallacies about vivisection"* assuming that the proposition most accepted *'is that the infliction of pain is in some cases justifiable, but not in all'.* Considering the need of research involving experimenting on animals, for the purpose of the well being of humans, in respect of finding a cure for diseases might be justifiable. However such proposition is hard to justify and we are in a sort of dilemma.

When you sip your tea up to the last drop in your mug and lay the mug on the tray before you and relax back and sink into your seat, and if you have a sensitive nature, you cannot avoid and feel a certain melancholy at the thought of all the labour . . . toil . . . pain that have been required to provide you with few minutes of delight and self satisfaction. These reflections became more piteous, distressing still when you are eating thick slices of steak. Since our planet became capable of supporting life through generations for millions upon millions of years creatures have come into existence, to end at last upon a plate can only emphasise human arrogance. It may be that being unconcerned human feeling cannot venture beyond the moments while eating a steak. The fate of human being is rather curious to consider. If you observe the ordinary persons from all walks of life and think of the endless history behind them and the course of events through a long series of hazards and peril that brought them to this moment, one would think a huge significance must be attached to them. Perhaps ordained or follow a predetermined pass by a fate over which they have no control. Perhaps they exist in dynamical systems which somehow become chaotic, and totally unpredictable, or having a fractal dimension that reflects an infinite similarity.

During the thousands of years of wandering the modern humans began encountering a new really tough enemy. They began to encounter other Homo sapiens who, during emigration and relocation in other parts of the globe and settled into new territories developing their own languages and their own way of life. These encounters between these groups, all belong to imaginative Homo sapiens, battled each other, for thousands years right up to the present time, trying to gain dominance over the other. History and prehistory is full of these bloody wars and battles and there is no sign of letup in this deadly chaos, disorder, havoc, and turmoil. There has been a constant struggle to gain superiority over their enemies with new and better deadly technology. Warfare technology has become so sophisticated and deadly that mankind is now capable of destroying itself and possibly even the planet. The cruelty, barbarity, savagery and ruthlessness, of modern human are beyond descriptions. In his poems on slavery Longfellow wrote to William Channing (who campaigned against slavery in America):

Well done! Thy words are great and bold;
At times they seem to me
Like Luther's, in the days of old,
Half-battles for the free.

Go on, until this land revokes
The old and chartered Lie,
The feudal curse, whose whips and yokes
Insult humanity.

Write! And tell out this bloody tale;
Record this dire eclipse,
This day of Wrath, this Endless Wail,
This dread Apocalypse!

He went on describing the long way to hell, of the victims forced into slavery.

Beside the ungathered rice he lay,
His sickle in his hand;
His breast was bare, his matted hair
Was buried in the sand.
Again, in the mist and shadow of sleep,
He saw his Native Land.

Mohamed M. Yousif

Wide through the landscape of his dreams
The lordly Niger flowed;
Beneath the palm-trees on the plane
Once more a king he strode;
And heard the tinkling caravans
Descend the mountain-road.

He saw once more his dark-eyed queen
Among her children stand;
They clasped his neck, they kissed his cheeks,
They held him by the hand!
A tear burst from the sleeper's lids,
And fell into the sand.

And then at furious speed he rode
Along the Niger's bank;
His pride-rein were golden chains,
And, with a martial clank,
At each leap he could feel his scabbard of steel Smiting
his stallion's flank.

Before him, like a blood-red flag,
The bright flamingos flew;
From morn till night he followed their flight,
O'er plains where the tamarind grew,
Till he saw the roofs of Caffre huts,
And the ocean rose to view.

At night he heard the lion roar,
And the hyenas scream,
And the river-horse, as he crushed the reeds
Beside some hidden stream;

And it passed, like a glorious roll of drums,
Through the triumph of his dream.
The forests, with their myriad tongues,
Shouted of liberty;
And the blast of the desert cried aloud,
With a voice so wild and free,
That he started in his sleep and smiled,
At their tempestuous glee.

He did not feel the driver's whip,
Nor the burning heat of day;
For death had illumined the land of sleep,
And his lifeless body lay
A worn-out fetter, that the soul
Had broken and thrown away!
All the things above were bright and fair,
All the things were glad and free;
Lithe squirrels darted here and there,
And wild birds filled the echoing air
With songs of liberty!

On him alone was the doom of pain,
From the morning of his birth;
On him alone the curse of Cain
Fell, like a flail on the garnered grain,
And struck to the earth!
. . .
In the ocean's wide domain,
Half buried in the sand,
Lie skeletons in chains,
With shackled feet and hands.
. . .

These are the bones of Slaves;
They gleam from the abyss;
They cry from yawning waves,
"We are the Witnesses!"
. . .
And oft the blessed time foretells
When all men shall be free;
And musical, as silver bells,
Their falling chains shall be.

Alas; but the cruelty among human, to this day, remained as before. I spent a lot of precious time reading and watching the news on the conflict nowadays, and the uprising of the masses against the tyrant rulers, who came to power by military means or rigged or manipulated the election or inherited the rule, ignored the masses robbed the wealth. Then they glued to their offices, feeling Invincible, till death removed them and even after death they continued ruling through their sons or relatives. Once they seized power, their love of money displays exactly characteristics as gangrene, for gangrene, once established in a body, never rests until it has invaded and corrupts the whole of it. To secure their power, they devised a brutal way of oppressing their citizens by all means. The army and the police forces were equipped to put down any resistance to their authority or even to protest against the miserable situation of the masses daily life. After exposing oneself to such events you develop Insomnia. And you keep roaming along the tiny space available by your dwelling . . . like in a cage and finally collapse from exhaustion and lay dozing for a little while. It is in vain to torment oneself over suffering that one cannot alleviate.

I proceeded making my way through the human wave. The square was getting in full swing of all sorts of activities . . . musicians, singers, painters. Beside the cathedral a row of Fiakers, an elegant carriage, a driver with a bowler hat and two beautiful horses at the head of each carriage, were getting ready to take tourist to roam through the inner City. The horses I noticed, as one day indicated by a friend I used to accompany him touring the city centre, had one of their front legs with the hoof few inches above the ground and after a couple of minutes in this position exchanged to the other leg and this would go on and on . . . as if to release the frustration they endured during their ordeal. At the square, you threaded your way among the holiday makers; a crowd of an unimaginable assortment of people . . . some were fat, old, ugly, stumpy, imbecilic, odd and stank . . . some were young elegant . . . charming . . . elderly couples hand in hand they looked so alike, with astonishing resemblance, it seemed through the course of years of marriage and being together so long, they acquired such resemblance. Japanese with their cameras filming every inch in all directions and their speech sounded like the twittering of birds. Groups from all over Europe, a mixture of many languages . . . Arabs from the Gulf states with their fat women in Khimar, a black long dress which covered them down to their toes and front and back and arms till wrist and covering their faces except for tiny holes for the eyes blinking in every direction . . . they looked like walking tents . . . following their men few steps behind . . . their teen children wearing western fits . . . tied Jeans and tied blouses showing their body lines . . . their interest was focused on the shops rather than the historical buildings of the city. A group of Italians full of charm and joy conversing with the aid of their hands and feet all together, you wondered who was listening to whom. Another elderly group was following a flag carrier, directing their route through the town. A small band, a guitarist, a blind fiddler, a harpist and wizards performing magic tricks and each had a plate or an open case before him to collect coins given by the spectators. Noisy young, group of Americans showing their talent in acrobatic dances to the rhythm of rap music. They attracted a quite large number of people. Painters drawing portraits for tourists or exhibiting their painting of Vienna known historical buildings in water colours, like the Rat House, theatres, Hofburg, parliament building, belvedere, burgtheater, opera, and Schoenbrunn. The most fascinating was a puppeteer manipulating a Marionette or "string puppet" . . . controlled by a number of strings, attached to his fingers and with an unusual expertise controlled the movements of the puppet and at the same time letting a chosen music in harmony with puppet playing a piano or a guitar. It was fantastic to observe especially most attractive for the children. A group of young ladies were wearing t-shirts reflecting at the back, 'Der letzte Tag der Freiheit' meaning the last day of freedom. I ventured and asked them the meaning of their campaign. They were gay and beautiful. They told me one of them was entering into matrimony the next day and they were sheering and laughing. The one who was renouncing her past and entering into the mysterious future, approached me and kissed me and asked if I could buy one or two tokens, she was holding, for a couple of Euros for a party to celebrate the occasion, which I did with great enthusiasm. I asked the bride to be, weather she prepared her trousseau. She grinned and said 'ya . . . ya . . . more or less'. I retuned her kiss and I lingered few seconds longer, she got excited hugged me and slipped away with a pleasant smile. The group went on laughing and singing. From where I was, I heard a Mozart melody streaming through the crowd and I headed towards it. A young Japanese lady surrounded by a crowd of people, was playing on her piano a Mozart piano concertos seeping through her fingers like a wave penetrating your soul. Music is the rhythm of the soul, and every tone, is synchronized with the natural vibration of your body. This lady playing; took me back through time when Mozart composed and played and sent heavenly melodies to the world around.

I headed towards the Bermuda Triangle situated in one of the oldest areas of Vienna, where was once the eastern part of the Roman Legion camp Vindobona, which was a Celtic Settlement on the Danube. At the Pedestrians Crossing a crowd of people on opposite sides waiting impatiently to cross watching the traffic light to turn green bending stretched their necks and part of their upper body towards the other side and the cars speeding through this arch of people persistently though some being impatiently gathered speed ran through whenever there was a gap between the following chain of cars. Some like a flock of sheep pre-programmed to the traffic lights move on only when the green light came on. Some were chatting unaware of the lights wanted to cross over but at last moment yelling pulling one another back and shouting . . . 'Hey the bloody light not green yet'. A number of pubs and concentration of catering spread along both sides of the street and crowded with customers chatting and enjoining their drinks. I wonder how many of them were aware that those streets witnessed the so called "Crystal Night" the night of broken glass, or "Kristallnacht" in German, which was an anti-Jewish pogrom, when in 1938, Nazi storm troopers plundered

Jewish homes, marauded through them, broke windows of Jewish-owned stores and looted merchandise, set fire to synagogues, and arrested many people. The broken glass, from windows and façade of the shops, strewn through the streets, was given the term "Crystal Night". Afterward the Lyric went on to express deeply felt emotion:

"Why—why do we turn away
When they shout that hymn
Marching so brave
Their hearts beat on boldly right
Their souls belong to those of the weak

Walking so blinded
Surrounded by brown coated lies
Hear propaganda which says
Bleed for the master race

We're not under the same nation
The past has gone—don't fear the new
It's your only chance—your only salvation

Why should we blond and blue-eyed
Chanting a 'heil'—living a lie
Evil surrounds us—we lost our way
Darkness will lead us through fire and hell

We're not waving the same flag
Or going down the same road
So use your brains—just for one time
You can't rule mankind

We're not under the same nation
The past has gone—don't fear the new
It's your only chance—your only salvation

No no we don't want it—never more
We won't take it—like before
Crystal night—never more

Never more—like before
No never more"

Back towards the Square I proceeded to the exclusive shopping street of Graben. The Graben or the ditch (Der Graben) goes back to Roman times. Originally the Romans had the fortress ditch of their camp in Graben. Later the place became a market for meat, vegetables and bread. The Column of the Black Plague (Pestsäule), a baroque architectural sculpture, in Graben was donated by the emperor Leopold I, during the terrible plague epidemic of 1679. On top of the sculpture one would observe a kind of clouds, angels and at the base the "Praying emperor".

At a side street off Graben I reached Café Havelka, one of my preference places in the city, where one could really relax and took a long deep breath. The warm and peaceful atmosphere of the coffee house became attractive for writers, painters and intellectual. From the pile of the news papers, provided by the coffee house for their customers, I selected one and proceeded and took a seat waiting for my friend. I ordered a cup of coffee and I was served in the original Viennese style, with the coffee brought on a small wooden tray with a small glass of water and a napkin on the side. The size of the Viennese newspapers, unlike those of other countries, was small and in away very convenient to hold and read just like reading a large book. I glanced at the first page reflecting what was happening in the world briefly and gave up before my depression reached its maximum. It seemed that one was doomed to be exposed to pain and agony from all sources—the brutality of the news and the horrid violence, killing and death. Even among kids; as old as twelve years; stabbing one another in the school reflecting the pessimistic destiny of our wretched generation. The news still reflecting on the monster Josef Fritzl who imprisoned, his teenage daughter, in an underground bunker, for twenty-four years. He raped and abused her and never letting her or the seven children she bore him, out of windowless cellar. That all happened in the small Austrian town of Amstetten. One would hardly perceive that such horror was going on for a quarter of a century in a tiny town, and no soul noticed. In 1984, Josef Fritzl asked his teen aged daughter, Elisabeth, into the basement of the family home under the claim that he needed help carrying a door. The door was the last piece needed to seal the bunker. Elisabeth held it in place while her father Josef got it into its frame. When it was fitted Josef held an ether-soaked towel on Elisabeth's face until she was unconscious. He threw her in the bunker after the door was fitted. In the following few days, he forced his daughter to write a letter, that she was staying with a friend and would not like to live with her family any more. When her mother reported to the police that her daughter was missing, her father told police that he suspected that his daughter had most likely joined a religious sect. One month later, her father handed over a letter—he forced his daughter to write, and later he posted to his address from another town—to the police, claiming that his daughter sent it.

The first few weeks Elisabeth desperately banged on the walls of the bunker and crying without avail. During the course of the following 24 years, Fritzl visited her in the hidden cellar every three days on average, to bring food and other supplies. He repeatedly had sexual intercourse with his daughter and had done so against her will. Elisabeth gave birth to seven children during her captivity. One child died shortly after birth, and three were removed from the cellar as infants to live with Fritzl and his wife. The Fritzls became the three children's foster parents with the knowledge of local social services authorities. Fritzl claimed that he found the three infants at his doorstep and that they were his grandchildren from his daughter Elizabeth. Nothing aroused the local authorities' suspicions.

The other three children remained in the cellar with their mother. Elisabeth taught the children to read and write.

In the year 2008, Kerstin, the eldest daughter, fell unconscious, and Josef Fritzl agreed to seek medical care. Elisabeth helped Fritzl carry Kerstin out of the cellar and saw the outside world for the first time in 24 years. She was then pushed back to the cellar by her father. Kerstin was taken by ambulance to a local hospital and admitted in serious condition with life-threatening kidney failure. Fritzl later arrived at the hospital claiming to have found a note written by Kerstin's mother. He discussed Kerstin's condition and the note with the Medical staff, who alerted the police when their suspicions increased listening to the story told by Fritzl. The police then appealed via public media for the missing mother to come forward. While the police was investigating, Elizabeth pleaded with her father to be taken to the hospital. Fritzl released Elisabeth from the cellar along with her two sons and told his wife that Elisabeth had decided to come back after a 24-year absence. Fritzl and Elisabeth went to the hospital where Kerstin was being treated. The police detained them on the hospital grounds and took them to a police station for questioning.

Elisabeth did not provide police with more details until they promised her that she would never have to see her father again. Then, she told the incredible story of her 24 years in captivity. Josef Fritzl confessed to having imprisoned his daughter for 24 years and having fathered her seven children. He was jailed for life.

I soon got bored with the paper and laid it down on the table. I looked around; the seated customers young and middle age absorbed in intimate talk puffing at their cigarettes and chatting some seriously some laughing and the smoke filled the place. Some busy with mobiles or MP3 hooked to their ears and swinging to the rhythm of the music. While sipping my coffee a fellow approached and politely asked whether he could share my table and I motioned him to take a chair and welcomed him. 'Danki' he said, and sank into the chair. The waiter came and he ordered coffee. He started conversing in English. He was one of those habitual frequenters of the place. He was between 40 or fifty dressed in grey shirt and a pair of grey trousers none too clean and on his feet he wore dusty boots. He had a long face, thin lips and blue eyes. His hair scattered on his head and forehead never been brushed. He had the quick movement of a bird. He was such an eternal talker, stopped only in exhaustion and had me at his mercy. He talked incessantly. He showed me a draft of a booklet he authored. 'You know, I could not to this day, find a publisher . . . they are so stupid can't appreciate the knowledge I conveyed in this book'. He was extremely vexed and started explaining his theory and philosophy contained in his book about the creation and the astronomy depicted by rather complex diagrams. I showed my concern and my sympathy to his cause. He soon jumped to another topic. 'I like this place and very often I come here . . . it is very nice . . . do you also like it' he said. I confirmed. He was very pleasant social fellow it seemed. He was one of those who had the gift of being able to jump over the first difficult phases of acquaintance and you had not known him for few minutes before you felt you had known him all his life. He gave me a couple of pages of his book to keep and read in my spare time and added in a mock humour jumping yet to another topic "this is a terrible world we are living in . . . war . . . war and war . . . conflicts and conflicts . . . never ending and who suffers . . . the poor people . . . you know who said . . . 'in war the strong make slaves of the weak, and in peace the rich make slaves of the poor'.'' He said. 'Oscar Wilde and very true' I said. 'ya . . . ya very true . . . perhaps one day it will be better . . . you see I sometimes tend to be optimistic' he said with a sarcastic smile. 'Have a good time and see you another time, take care my friend.' He said. 'You too' I said. He excused himself and left. I ordered another cup of tea and relaxed waiting for my friend. Regretfully, many of such cafés were being replaced by MacDonald's fast food chain restaurants and I wondered how long this one would last.

Part 3

Of all the animals, man is the only one that lies.
Mark Twain

Many roads lead to riches. And most are dirty.

The goddess of fortune is not only blind themselves, but usually it also makes those blind, has ensnared them. Greed caused all crimes and misdeeds.

CICERO

My friend arrived and I greeted him warmly enquiring about family and friends back home. 'All Tamam' he said. The word, 'Tamam' meant gratification, contentment and satisfaction and was very much used back home and one would hear it many times over and over whenever people met and conversed with each other. They uttered the word 'Tamam' even if it was followed by complains such as life was intolerable and things were worst than last year. As usual my friend started his conversation with politics and how things became dreadful and beyond any imagination. He was a tall slim fellow fair complexion. He started describing the capital city back home and how incredible it was, a big mess and millions of people going about the city struggling for their living. People from rural areas, migrated to the capital seeking jobs. Thousands of foreigners from neighbouring countries and countries as far as India and Sri Lanka were pouring into the capital for the same purpose. The traffic jam created unusual city commerce by the side road mixing with the traffic. Many were peddlers carrying all kinds of merchandise one can imagine; toys, tool kits, clothing, Mangoes, oranges, bananas, pencils, spare parts of all kinds, radios, batteries, and many more low quality articles from China, Korea. Patiently bargaining with the drivers; and since the slowness of the traffic was so predictable they leave their merchandizes with the drivers and follow, knowing that the traffic will jams few meters further and they would continue the bargaining. The peddlers would usually pay more attention to the most privileged drivers of the latest model cars like Mercedes and BMW which surprisingly were many on the streets of the city. For the majority of people who work in the city, the bus was the only means of transport in city and beyond. The traffic was a nightmare. Most of the buses star at AbueGinzeer square, named after a holy man. The square was a melting pot of people, a labyrinth of nations from all over the country as well as from neighbouring countries as far as Nigeria, central Africa, and Burkina Faso. Haggling; in the moving Souk in the square and beyond, an experience beyond any sensible imagination. It was easy to get lost in labyrinthine hustle of disoriented moving mass of people—and just as easy to lose your way in a haggling contest with a peddler for whom bargaining was a way of life. One was confronted with beggars and cripples at every turning in the square. The buses lined in this square in a queue. The bus at the head of the queue had to be filled in with the passengers to the point that any further passenger would fall off. Passengers on the route of bus beyond the square have no chance of embarking unless by luck a passenger would disembark. No bus stations on the route were known, so if a passenger would like to disembark somewhere along the route he or she must flick two fingers or snap his fingers like a school kid in class and the driver hearing the flick would stop and let the passenger to disembark. If the driver was too busy or the cassette recorder by his side was too loud to hear the flick, the ticket collector would whistle or make a sound like Shi . . . Shi . . . and the driver would make an abrupt stop. The ticket collector was not a real ticket collector for there were no tickets to collect but rather collecting cash money. The seating of the passengers was a hindrance to the money collector, as the middle passage was occupied by passengers on collapsible seats, but never the less he would manage by leaning on the passengers of the first and second row as far as his stretch would allow him to reach as many passengers as possible and snap his fingers as a sign to demand payment. For some unknown phenomenon his snap of his fingers would not arouse the driver or prompt him to stop . . . so there must be a distinction between his and the passenger. The passengers at the back would hand their payment to the passengers in the next row and so on so forth to the hands of the collector who would then keep the money between his fingers. Sometimes the bus driver would suddenly divert from his route and head to a petrol station to refill ignoring the safety of passengers on the bus.

We laughed at his tale, but with distress and pity. We recalled, the good old days in the capital. Yes it used to be so clean and quiet . . . few people . . . no beggars . . . all well dressed clean people and when we used to go down town in the evenings most of the people you met on the streets or cafes or restaurants you would know by name. We ordered another round of tea and coffee. We continued reminisces of our home. My friend recalled the fabulous time when the capital used to receive tourists from Europe, during the holiday seasons of Christmas and New Year. And how the town used to receive them; with all splendid charm in places like Atini, Coupacopana, Acropol St James, high standard Hotels, just to mention few. The souk Alafrangi (this was an exclusive elegant shopping area) with its attractive shops was a dream to the unlucky ones of today. None would imagine or envisage the downfall to be so fast to the degree of reversing such high standards to such miserable situation in a short span of time. Nothing left except Ruin, desolation, and annihilation. 'Ah' we both thought. 'Would those prosperous days return once more?'

Part 4

'The witness swore on the holly Book,
To tell the truth,
But told lies and nothing but lies.
The judge weary let it pass.
The defendant full of disgust,
Watching . . .'

My friend who was always interesting in the behaviour of human and the causes of a particular behaviour, wanted to indulge even at the risk of running into unpleasant situations. This time he was adamant to find out how certain individuals behave and why in this particular peculiar incident. The incident involved interesting characters of all walks of life. Lawyers, police, drivers, mechanics, a judge, and other individuals not connected with the incident but suffered similar cases. He was well aware; one would never know everything about human nature though in this case the economic motive was the driving force. People's character was self-contradictory and haphazard bundle of inconsistent qualities. I shall attempt to narrate the story he told, in my own words. His friend had a car accident with no injury involved, which would have been a normal car accident to be resolved by the insurance companies without the police involvement. Sadly the other car had no insurance and the driver insisted it was not his fault and would like to settle things and suggested a certain amount of money to be paid for him to repair his car without involving the police. The police who happened to be there at the time of accident concurred with him and advised that the mattered should be resolved by payment. But our friend refused to do that and therefore was compelled to face the traffic court or so he had chosen.

The proceeding of the traffic court was set for the next day. To relieve himself he decided to spend the evening along the Nile. He strolled along the Nile Avenue, passing the Grand Hotel and, on the right, Toti Island across the Blue Nile. It seemed to him the island was becoming closer to the bank on his side. A cool breath touched his face, relieving him from the hot still air of the town. The clear dark sky was increasingly illuminated by blinking, scattered stars. The confluence of the Niles was moving up the Blue Nile almost in line with the Grand Hotel, for the waters of the White Nile were pushing in the direction of the blue waters as if in a hurry to embrace and mix with their gentle waves before the usual meeting point below Omdurman Bridge. The distinct colours of the waters were clear to the eye; blue and brownish and then further on, they mixed forming the Nile in their journey to the north. Further down on the Blue Nile few sailing boats scattered on the surface sailing lazily around. He recalled how, when he was strolling during a similar evening, along Shambat Bridge from Khartoum north across the Nile to Omdurman, and when resting at the barrier of the Bridge looking towards Omdurman Bridge, he would see such spectacular scenery, a landscape so beautiful that he would linger there for hours.

Next day he proceeded to building where the traffic court was housed. In the court room; the judge who presided over the case, known as Mawalana, was a large man with a face as black as ebony. He was glued to his chair in a way you would think he would not part from it. He had a fleshy face with large black eyes. He had a large bold skull. He wore a full grey suit, white shirt and unmatched blue tie. His dress was ill-suited to the hot weather and you would observe that he was drenched with sweat, which he wiped constantly with a handkerchief. He spoke with a high pitched voice. He frowned and looked very severe. He presided over his court whenever his time would allow. Most of the time, he never showed up despite the lawyers, witnesses who waited for hours for him to appear. At the very end of the day a message would be delivered by a police man telling the waiting crowd that Mawalana might show up tomorrow inshaa Allah, if God will.

The lawyers, representing the owner of the car, Oman2 and Oman1, both are small fellows, dwarf with the colour of cold asphalt. Both were uncivil. It is hard to believe or comprehend that they would be to any school to qualify for the profession they claim to work for. Oman2 was like a bushman, dusty with a sallow face and a narrow weak chin, snub nose and shaggy eyebrows. His partner Oman1 had an unhealthy pale look dreadful fellow. He had small and undistinguished features and his expression was artless. Both were extremely greedy, with hungry look and strived to earn money by all means through cheating or whatever means and dirty manipulation of circumstances in their favour. When they saw the money completely inhibited their ability and power of conversation. Most probably they did not qualify for a law degree, but somehow they manipulated their way to be lawyers by illegal methods. In this respect my friend mentioned that a guy who impersonated a medical doctor; worked in a hospital for a couple of years before he was unveiled. For a lawyer such a deceit would be less harmful, but a medical doctor it was a catastrophic. The lawyer representing the insurance company was a small fat fellow with his necktie hanging from his neck sideways. He was of the same category as the two lawyers. He rarely showed up before the court. The traffic police was slim and with hungry look. His legs were like broomsticks. His cheeks were hollow. He was deeply sunburned. His face looked tired but his expression was very gentle. When he walked, you got the idea of a dead leaf dancing before the wind. Like many policemen he was most probably under paid. A witness was a mechanic. He was a large plump man and one of those who learned the names of car parts by heart but lacked the knowledge of their functions. The Car owner was a fat hobbling fellow, broad and stout. His testimony was a load of lies. Swearing, on the holy book, to tell the truth, played no role and won't persuade him to tell the truth. An engineer by profession was behaving like any peddler on the street.

The so called traffic court was situated within a huge building in the mid of the busiest traffic area of the city. It was a busy junction of four main streets. The junction was a roundabout junction. At the entrance of the building a traffic police in his white dress sat on a chair chatting with someone who gave him a snuff which he placed between his lower lip and teeth, followed by a spit on the ground before him. A woman was brewing tea for some customers who were sitting on the ground around her. She half filled a tea cup with sugar before adding the hot tea over and handed it to the customer who noisily drank his tea. She had a bucket, half full of water sprinkled with detergent soap, beside her, which was handy to wash used cups, these were inserted in the bucket to rinse for a split-second, pulled out a number of cups held by her fingers, and dried them by a piece of cloth. She repeated the process of washing for as long as it took her before finishing her job for the day, without bothering to change the water. Beside her a boy was selling cigarettes. Cigarettes were sold as single cigarette or a box of ten cigarettes each. Peddlers passing by were carrying all kinds of merchandise one can imagine; toys, tool kits, pencils, spare parts of all kinds, radios, batteries, and many more low quality articles from China, Korea. A police man was chasing the peddlers to clear the area and they scampered, only to return again when the police went to exercise his job on the other side of the street or to relax when exhausted from the chase. A blind man led by a small boy whined and wailed endlessly for demand for alms.

The traffic court was in a shabby section of the building. The judges or Mawalana, as they were known occupied four rooms in a row, with their names written on top of each door. Outside each door they were two dusty wooden benches, good for five people only, while hundreds of people waiting outside had to roam the small place beyond the benches waiting for Mawalanas. The dust lay heavy on the rim of closed windows at the back of the benches. Nobody knew when the Mawalanas would arrive and take their benches. At half pass nine the police and others working for the court would disappeared for a long break to enjoy their breakfast followed by several cigarettes or a snuff and a cup of tea. Till then everything would stand still. The small canteen serving breakfast for the staff of the court, visitors and others from neighbouring offices could hardly cope with the crowd. After breakfast, reluctantly and slowly they return to their jobs, after a lapse of a minimum of two hours.

It was indeed a bizarre affair watching what was happening just like a comedy play on which a ridiculous act was performed. Most of the cases, not involving injuries, could have been settled out of the court between insurance companies! Like in most if not all of the countries of the world. It seemed that the system was designed to invite corruption of the lawyers, witnesses and the under paid police. The court proceedings went on very slow listening to all kind of witnesses, though the defendant admitted his fault and just was waiting to pay the penalty, which was a nominal value since his insurance would cover the rest. Never the less it went on and on for the lawyers Oman1 and Oman2 wanted to press the defendant to pay them. They even went to the extent of asking the defendant to pay a certain sum and they would pullout from the case. The defendant utterly refused, but the case went on and on for a couple of weeks and at the end he gave up, after being exhausted and had no more time to waste, and paid the greedy lawyers a sum of money as a compensation to the car owner provided that they would withdraw their claim from the court. The defendant made the mistake of not getting any signed paper from the lawyers that he paid them on the understanding that they would withdraw from the case. The next day they asked the judge to announce his judgment on the case which was that the defendant would pay the nominal penalty. In that case obviously the defendant, assuming the promise the lawyers, would get his money back from the lawyers, they promised to do that, but to this day they refused to pay. His friend was really very furious, though he managed to get a written paper from Oman1 that he would get his money back. But, alas, he did not get a single penny.

Part 5

I suffer at the hands of despotic rulers;
I suffered slavery under insane invades;
I suffer hunger imposed by tyranny;
Yet, I still possess some inner power
With which I struggle to greet each day.

Kahlil Gibran

How heavy do I journey on the way,
When what I seek, my weary travel's end,
Doth teach that case and that repose to say,
"Thus far the miles are measured from thy friend!"
The beast that bears me, tired with my woe,
Plods dully on, to bear that weight in me,
As if by some instinct the wretch did know
His rider loved not speed being made from thee.
The bloody spur cannot provoke him on
That sometimes anger thrusts into his hide,
Which heavily he answers with a groan,
More sharp to me than spurring to his side;
For that same groan doth put this in my mind:
My grief lies onward and my joy behind.

William Shakespeare

M_y friend went on narrating the following episode relating to an acquaintance by the name of Zool:

Zool stretched his aching legs on a chair which he pulled close to the bench where he was sitting. With his shaky hands he pulled a letter from his pocket which he read over hundred times . . . he received only the day before . . . could not believe or comprehend the meaning of the words in his brain . . . it went on saying *"for the reason of public interest or commonweal your services are no longer needed"*. It was very hot and the drops of sweat from his forehead were increasing. Neither illness nor lassitude prevented him from going on with his work. For more than twenty years he toiled unremittingly. To be treated so contumeliously and taking revenge on him was like depriving the country of the vast accumulation of knowledge he acquired, which was lost forever and deprived him and his family of their income to face an unknown future and jeopardizing their existence. So he was sacked from his job for the 'commonweal'; for the sake of his country. 'Bastards' he thought. All the years he toiled and now he was pulled clean like a hair out of the Dough. Such letter was rather common among many of his acquaintances and associates who were unlawfully kicked out of their jobs for political reasons or for not siding with the regime or had history of being against any totalitarian regimes, thus thousands lost their jobs and those who showed slightest resistance were thrown in jails and endured the inhumane torture within 'Buat-alashbah', ghost houses, a special prison for torturing political prisoners. The designation 'ghost houses' was because interrogators were veiled when they were torturing prisoners in the homes of police secret service, and used false names to call each other. They were sadist and barbarians.

Our friend Zool reflected on this and thought his situation compared with the others, was the least unfortunate. His immediate boss, then director, was sacked a couple of month before him. Being his deputy Zool was expected to follow his boss any time after the new director was in place. He foresaw and had been certain that his dismissal from employment was imminent. He would not tolerate the new director any way for he was incompetent and unfit for the job as he lacked the suitable qualification. He was a political appointee. Zool thought awhile scratched his head lit a cigarette and started to consider seriously his family future and the options available. Firstly he had to struggle for his pension and then thought of possibilities of earning some income to elevate the hardship awaiting him. His priority was set for his three kids in school their fees plus the daily expenses. Tough times waiting ahead. In his time education was free, medical care was free and life was not that expensive.

The mirage shone before his eyes and the fantasy held them for sometimes through bleaks of happiness! He thought of buying a second hand rickshaw to roam the streets to earn some money . . . . He heard many stories how useful a rickshaw could be. These bloody rickshaws were imported from India by some of those bloodsucking new millionaires. We never had any such a thing before he thought.

The capital limits marked the effective borders of the country, outside these borders the official life was nonexistent, for the capital was where all the money flows and the place where there was any hope of finding a job.

The capital was attracting more job seekers to the extent that it became impossible to find any job. Nevertheless they desperately survive by peddling, stealing and begging. Some of those employed by the government were obliged to accept bribes, in order to perform their duties, as the pay was not sufficient. Zool, unlike many, was an honest and trustworthy fellow and lived within his income. Zool succeeded in acquiring a rickshaw and tried for a couple of weeks to drive it through the streets himself but soon he gave up . . . too old to manage such alien job so he was advised to hire a boy. At the end of the day the boy would bring to him a certain agreed sum of money. Few years later he looked older and miserable from the burden of life never the less he strived on and on and life was a bit at his finger ends when he died. The body that he, had treated so contumeliously took its revenge on him.

That vast accumulation of knowledge from his job was lost forever. To the world he was unknown in death as he was in life. And yet he was a success. He did what he wanted honestly, tried to adjust to his new situation and he died when his goal was in sight and never knew the bitterness of an end achieved.

Part 6

By the sidewalk,
I met a little girl
A sweet little girl
Her eyes more black and wide
But looking deep . . . deep
Into the lovely eyes
You wonder into a world of sadness.
A sweet little girl
Her age . . . six . . . ten can't tell.
Through her sadness
And through the lovely misty eyes
You can read a tale of a nation
A tale of suffer without measure,
A tale of agony without pleasure.
She smiled back to me
Holding firm
To what I gave
And melted in the crowd
Of many alike.

'The tremendous world I have in my head, but how free myself and free it without being torn to pieces. And a thousand times rather be torn to pieces than retain it in me or bury it.'
Kafka

At a junction leading to Boulaq district in Cairo, thousands of people gathered. The space in the middle was taken up by vendors displaying their merchandise on carts and tables right across a train rails. The place was crowded by buyers and peddlers. The train rails disappeared in the mob. I was standing there in amazement watching the crowd moving to and fro like ants and wandering what would happen if a train would show up . . . but then I thought that the rails might be deserted rails . . . but while I was speculating I heard a train whistle. I looked right and left and I saw at a distance not far from the mob a train was approaching . . . nearer and nearer but no one was in the least disturbed by the approaching train . . . I thought . . . oh my God a catastrophe would no doubt on the version of happening. Just when the train was a couple of meters away, the crowd of people like waves of sea, on both sides of the rail, opened up for the train to pass . . . . like when the waters of the red sea opened for Moses and his followers to cross, fleeing from Pharaoh soldiers. When the last wagon was passing away the waves of humans closed on the rail and business went as usual.

The writing behind public buses and rickshaws, in Khartoum, is quite interesting; it is a barometer of popular culture. They go to great lengths to have their machines personalized by lines depicting their sentiments expressed through poetry, quotations, and verses of the Qur'an or the sayings of Prophet Muhammad. The lines behind Buses, rickshaws, trucks and private cars, carry such immense philosophy—both personal and public—even for a casual observer. For me they reflect Songlines along the roads which convey the inner feelings of those toiling along the road to support their living and to survive the peril of life.

A similar situation I came across during my visit to Karachi in Pakistan, few years back. There it was spectacular to watch all kind of vehicles painted all over with colorful lines and background reflecting phrases like: *Good intention, Easy destination, Tolerance and patience are the principles of life, Gratitude to God, No one is faithful, I am not the owner God is, Just come once!, Only God Bestows, Hard target.*

Here are some examples *(on buses and rickshaws in Khartoum)*: (*I included the English translation beside the Arabic text*)

- غدار دموعك (*treachery of your tears*)

- اوعك تمشي في درب ما عارف دموعك (*never walk on a road which doesn't know your tears ... meant road of love*)

- العشق الممنوع (*the forbidden love*)

- الزنجيه (black)

- الدكتورة (*means female medical dr.*)

- حبيبة عُمرى *Habibat omry (popular song, my ever love)*.

- من غير ميعاد (*without* rendez vous)

- شايل جراح (*injured.*)

- سلام قول من رب رحيم)*peace from merciful God.*)

- موعود (*promised.*)

- فريدة من نوعها (*she is unique.*)

- ليمون بارا (*Bara lemon.*)

- رضاك يا أمي (*longing for mom satisfaction.*)

76

- القروش (*money.*)

- جراب الرأي (*opinion pouch .*)

- بدر الزمان (*moon of the time.*)

- ما تشيلي هم (*do not worry.*)

- أسمعنا مرة (*listen once.*)

- بتتعلم من الايام (*learn from days*)

- علي طول الطريق (*along the way.*)

- ما شاء الله (*God will.*)

- تبارك الله (*Blessed God.*)

- يا دنيا اه (*ah! World.*)

- نفسي اقطع الكبري (*I wish I could cross the bridge*). *Rickshaws are not allowed to cross bridges.*

Franz Kafka's Metamorphosis.

Gregor Samsa, was a travelling salesman. He knew how depressing and tedious life as a travelling salesman was. Had it not been for his family dependant on his income, he would have quitted his job. His father lost his business, he was ill and his sister could not afford to pay for her studies in music. Gregor had plans for his sister to help her and he was waiting to surprise her and announce on Christmas day to send her to study at the Conservatorium. He hated his chief and he was adamant to pay back his parents' debt to him and free himself. Then he settled in his tiny room to sleep with all these thoughts developing in his brain. In the morning he woke up to find himself transformed into a giant insect. Bewildered, he looked around his room which he found normal. He decided to fall asleep again and forget what happened to him in the hope that condition will revert back to normal. He tried to roll over to his right but discovers that he cannot due to his new body—he was stuck on his hard, arched back. He tried to touch his stomach but his numerous legs were moving in uncontrollable directions. He realized that he had overslept missed his train for work. Gregor never been late for his work and his mother knocks on his door to see what was wrong. He answered her but his voice had changed and she thought that he might be ill. His sister, Grete, came to his door and begged him to open the door. He tried to get out of bed but being incapable of moving his body in his new condition he failed. In the mean time his office manager came to check up on him and was at his door urging him to open the door and warned him of the consequences of missing his work. He added that Gregor recent performance had been unsatisfactory. Gregor finally out of bed fell to the floor and called out that he would open the door shortly. Gregor was unaware that his voice had been transformed thus none of persons on the other side of the door could understand a single word he uttered. Finally,

Gregor managed, after a great effort, to use his mouth to unlock and open the door. All shocked by the sight of Gregor's appearance. His mother fainted. The manager fled out of the apartment. Gregor tried to creep toward him trying to hold him back, but his father drove him back into his room with a cane. Gregor squeezed back through the doorway, injuring himself and his father slammed the door shut. Gregor, exhausted, fell asleep. His family bewildered confused did not know how to cope with the situation. Gregor woke up and found milk and bread in his room. He could touch the milk, though it was once one of his favourite drinks. He settled himself under the couch. The next morning, his sister came and found out he had not touched the milk and replaced it with leftover food, which Gregor happily ate. His sister took the task of feeding him and cleaning up while he hid under the couch. Gregor was listening through the wall to his family members talking. Amazingly he understood them, though the words were faintly coming to his ears. They often discussed the difficult financial situation they found themselves in now; since Gregor would not be able to provide for them. His mother wanted to visit him, but his sister and father would not let her. Gregor got more used to his new situation and started climbing the walls and ceiling. His sister decided to remove some of the furniture to give Gregor more space. She and her mother began taking furniture away, but Gregor did not like that. He tried to save a picture he liked. Gregor's mother saw him hanging on the wall and fainted and collapsed. Grete upset shouted at him and Gregor—finding the door opened crawled fast out and into the kitchen. At this moment his father returning from his new job, faced with this situation thought that Gregor attacked the mother. The father threw apples at Gregor, and one hit his back and remained lodged there. Gregor managed to get back into his bedroom but was severely injured. Gregor's family decided to leave his door open for a few hours each evening so that he could watch them. He realized his family wearing down as a result of his transformation and their new poverty. Even Grete seems to resent Gregor. The family replaced their maid with a cheap cleaning lady who tolerates Gregor's appearance and spoke to him occasionally. To compensate for the lost loss of income Gregor used to provide, the family took in three boarders requiring them to move excess furniture into Gregor's room, which distresses Gregor. Eventually Gregor lost his taste for the food and he almost entirely ceased eating. One evening, the cleaning lady left Gregor's door open while the boarders were in the living room, enjoying the music played by Grete.

Gregor crept out of his bedroom to listen. The boarders, who initially seemed interested in Grete, grow bored with her performance, but Gregor is transfixed by it. One of the boarders saw the huge insect creping and got alarmed. The boarders protested and announced that they would move out immediately without paying rent because of the disgusting conditions in the apartment. After such an incident, his sister suggested to get rid of Gregor otherwise they would all be ruined. Her father agreed. Gregor understood their situation crowed back to his room. Eventually, he died of stress, starvation and the injury caused by his father. Upon discovering the death of Gregor, the family felt a great sense of relief. The father got rid of the boarders and fired the cleaning lady, who disposed of Gregor's body. The family managed to make substantial savings and they decide to move to a better apartment. Grete appeared to have her strength and beauty back, which led her parents to think about finding her a husband.

Mr. **Arino was a man full of deceit.** Arino was the most pernicious, wicked person he ever met. The chaotic circumstances of life threw both within a team working for an organisation. Arino was a small fat bulky person, had a round protruding belly, looking like a clown in his boggy trousers. He was a chain smoker. His breath, when you come closer to him, smell like somebody intoxicated by alcohol. Indeed he was a heavy drinker. You loathe the very sight of him. He set to sabotage his colleagues work and claimed work achieved by them. He had his devious deceitful ways to achieve his unethical goals. It was not at all pleasant to work with him, though it was fair to say that Arino outside the former duties, sometimes he gave you the impression of a nice sociable person.

Marzogy **was a man without conscience.** Due to chaotic events in one's life, he met Marzogy on the street where he lived. An episode of no moment, that might easily not had happened, had repercussions that were inestimable. It looked as though blind chance rated all things. Marzogy a Middle height enormously stout, he had a large fleshy face with cheeks hanging on each side. After the usual greetings Marzogy started conversing about his plans to establish a centre for dialysis and he was looking for a house to lease for that purpose. He claimed that he was working in a dialysis centre in a foreign country for a number of years. He already procured all equipment necessary and just was looking for a suitable place. Marzogy asked him, whether he would be willing to lease his house. The house's owner told him he was very sorry he could not, though he was very sympathetic for his venture which was very much needed in the country at that time. Marzogy understood and said if he would ever change his mind he would be glad to take the house. Marzogy kept coming almost every day talking about his project and showed himself as a very genuine fellow and very keen to establish the centre to help people in need. Unfortunately the house owner yielded to Marzogi wish and agreed to lease his house. The house owner made the mistake of not enquiring into the back ground of Marzogy and his qualifications. Marzogy settled the first quarterly rent payment but never bother to make any further payments for almost a year during which he sublet the house to one of his relatives who set an office for a company. Subletting was illegal act and when the house owner faced him with this violation, Marzogy justified this by saying he was waiting for approval of the authorities to start the dialysis and would resume payment as soon as he got the approval to start installing the equipments. Officially Marzogy was not allowed to sublet the house, but going in a legal battle would take ages, so the house owner decided to wait. To make a long story short, two years passed during which Marzogy settled a meagre amount of payment. Then it turned out that Marzogy was using a solution for the separation of colloids not to the prescribed specifications. He was found out by the medical authorities and the centre was closed. Marzogy was the most insignificant that ever breathed and most crashing bore. It turned out that Marzogi was a Bus driver employed by dialysis centre somewhere abroad. This was about the only connection he had with dialysis. The owner got his house back in ruin, walls pulled down, doors and windows were missing and electric appliances were pulled out of walls. It was very sad that no further investigation were carried perhaps due to his connections with authorities . . . but it was a crime committed by Marzogy, strange though Marzogy was not in the least disturbed. He showed no concern and went on with his deviousness and deception. Perhaps Marzogy caused the death of innocent people or at least attempted murder. Any law on earth would have prosecuted him and put him behind bars for a number of years. Fortunately Marzogy deviousness and deception was then directed to less harmful ways, by adopting trade in the market selling and buying, though thieving is the cheapest most despicable act, short of murder, for money.

Part 7

I was Here from the moment of the
Beginning, and here I am still. And
I shall remain here until the end
Of the world, for there is no
Ending to my grief-stricken being.

I roamed the infinite sky, and
Soaring in the ideal world, and
Floated through the firmament. But
Here I am prisoner of measurement.

I heard the teaching of Confucius;
I listened to Brahma's wisdom;
I sat by Buddha under the Tree of Knowledge.
Yet here am I, existing with ignorance
And heresy.

Kahlil Gibran

His first cry completed manfully with the sand storm blowing fiercely over the hut. And the cold air filled his lungs fully giving his first breath. It was winter and the cold desert air blowing through the cracks in the window and the top funnel of the Hut (*Gotia*). His father inserted a *Quffah;*

*(Quffah is a common basket and used for carrying dates vegetables and other various household items) t*o the funnel to block incoming cold air. In the middle of the hut, a burning char coal on a *Mangad* was trying desperately to resist the incoming freezing air.

His birth was a great event in the village, when almost all of inhabitant of the village, men and women with their children came over dragging a number of sheep to slaughter to celebrate occasion, firing their guns as a welcome for the newly born. The newly born was later nicked named *WadalKohila*, the son of *Kohila,* named after *Kohila,* the tiny village in *Dar al-Manasir*, where he was born. It was a big celebration. The boy grew in this remote area in the Northern part of the country, *Dar al-Manasir*, by the river Nile, where his father worked for the railways maintaining a post at an isolated station, monitoring trains coming and leaving by recording type of train, date and time of arrival and departure and delivering information to the next station. The post also involved recording daily statistical data relating to the Nile level at that station, where the sand dunes extended almost touching the river. His father (Sheik Mahmoud Yousif) launched the first school ever in that part of the country. Before his father arrived to that part of the country there was a hundred percent illiteracy among the village population.

The boy, then five years old, taken by his mother to have a bath. She stripped him naked beside the huge water containers called *Fanateez* located adjacent to the railway track. His tiny body shivered to the sight of the water which seemed cold to him; though the sun heated the iron containers keeping the water inside warm enough for a bath. His mother started boring water over his body and scrubbing the dirt off with a bar of soap and . . . . he continued to cry and sob while she continued holding and scrubbing his body to remove the accumulated dirt off his skinny body . . . she felt as if his body was becoming more skinnier and at that thought she stopped and started to dry him up and gave him a motherly embrace and then she held him protectively in both hands and carried him back to the Hut. At home she pulled from under the bed a heavy metallic suitcase, opened it and removed a carefully folded new *Galabia (garment)* and *Surwal (under wear)*, unfolded them and dressed the boy. She watched him with his face radiating happiness . . . she smiled and kissed him and said "Eid mobarak` and added "These are new" pointing to his new dress "do not render them dirty or ruin them . . . good boy . . . tomorrow morning you shall wear them for the Eid". He responded with a bow of his head. He went to bed dreaming of the Eid and all the nice things . . . candy . . . especial food . . . play mates from the village . . . he dreamt of the long walk from their Hut with his father to the praying site . . . close by the river . . . the forbidden river for the young boys like him were not allowed to even approach it unaccompanied. They feared being drown or eaten by crocodiles.

The morning of the Eid the whole family got up very early and breakfast was served . . . tea with milk and his father added *Samna* in each cup of tea with a serious look to prevent any protest from his children.

Reluctantly the boy swallowed down his very fatty tea with a piece of Kisra, native bread. Nobody uttered a word except the words "eat and drink" coming from the father accompanied by a serious look and a frown.

He accompanied his father to Eid prayers (*Salat Al-Eid*). His father, Sheik Mahmoud, Whom he rarely looked into his face, was a great father and the boy often pitied other boys and would not comprehend that they did not have such great father. His father was very popular among the village population and even beyond . . . they came with their problems and disputes . . . seek his advice . . . they came when they were sick to seek treatment . . . they brought their children to the *Khalwa* to learn writing and reading and study Quran and thus observing prayers to be good Muslims. The boy looked so proud among other boys.

Eid was a great occasion when the village men gather at the burial place of a holy man named *Ahmed Elbadawi*, located not far from the river Nile. The prayer was led by his father Sheikh Mahmoud Yousif. The boy noticed that after the prayers all men rushed towards his father bowing before him and kissing his hand . . . to get his blessing. The children enjoyed the occasion too by their new clothes and the candy distributed by the elders to them. Afterwards the boy joined a couple of boys to play on the sand surrounding their resident till he was drowsy and was carried by his mother to his traditional bed called *Anqarib*.

The school or Khalwa, which was a religious school, in which Quran studies were taught, was a mixture of kids of five years and grown-ups up to fifteen years of age. They were taught reading and writing and some basic arithmetic. Once they were through the stage of being able to read and write they were introduced to learn religious lessons and memorizing short verse from Quran to observe prayers. Each pupil was given a slab made of wood called Looh to write on, this was a wooden panel smoothed and cleaned and then plaster with whitewash using chalk. The ink was prepared from a mixture of soot, taken from the lower part, where the accumulated soot caused by the burning wood to heat a hot plate called Doka used for preparing bread, this soot was then mixed with gum Arabic and water. The mixture gave a black ink called Amar which was then used for writing on the Looh. The writing pen was made from a piece of dry grass stems called Gasaba shaped and sharpened into a good writing point (nib) at one end which was then split in the middle to hold a small amount of ink and very often one would need to dip the writing point in the ink to write few words. A pupil, who would learn a pre-assigned part (Gozo) of the Quran, would be given an especial celebration called Sharafa. The last Surah of that Gozo was nicely written on the `Looh` with a colourful frame using the natural dyes and colours derived from plants and minerals in the area. On the day of the celebration everyone was expressing his happiness by jumping and running about and all congratulating each other and wishing to attain `Sharafa` as soon as possible. It was a great motivation for the pupils to be diligent in their studies. The elder students were then helped to find some sort of technical or vocational school where they could learn a profession within the railways work shops or similar jobs. Indeed many of them were successful in finding jobs and earned a reasonable income that helped their families and allowed them to send their children to schools, though away from home. The nearest town, miles away from their village, was Atbara, which was the headquarters of the railways, where jobs were available as well as schools. Those who managed were extremely grateful to this day.

Zainab Eldikeer came very often to visit them. They watched her walking from her hut down the hill of sand where her hut was located. She was rolling down like a ball from the top toward their resident. They were terribly excited watching and arguing whether the rolling figure was Zainab or some other figure. When the rolling ball was progressing nearer and took the shape of human, it was evident that the figure was Zainab, she was the only one living there after all. Zainab Eldikeer resembled an emblem of the tough living conditions engulfing the thin impoverished population round that area. The sand dunes reached and almost touching the river; barely leaving a thin fertile strip of land, which the people utilized to grow vegetables and some grass for their goats. Goats were raised for their milk a part of which is processed to produce butter (Samna). The process was rather simple. The process used a vessel made from goatskin for a churn. The goatskin was closed tight with a rope from one end and the milk was poured in from the other end and held tight from this end by hand, then the skin was suspended from a pole and swung to and fro several times until the butter was formed. The butter or Samna was then extracted from the skin. The remaining milk with a very low fat was poured in a bowl especially made from the hard outer shell of a fruit or gourd called Garaa which was also used as a drinking pot or container for liquids. The low fat milk, then called

Roub, was consumed as a drink. Zainab looked frail and exhausted. She cuddled a bottle of Samna. She smiled and offered the bottle to them. In her late forties she showed a face of somebody in his late sixties. Her face covered with wrinkles with the colour of the sand she was walking through. They invited her inside the courtyard of the only bed room. The room was built, from red bricks and cement, in a round shape of a hut with a protruding cone like roof, which later we called a rocket waiting to be launched. It was surprising and astonishing why the British came with such design, though no such shapes of building existed in that area. The colonial authorities never thought of including a sanitary system in these buildings. Though the river Nile was about one kilometre from railway station, water was supplied once a week or so by train. Three large containers (called Fanatiez) placed adjacent to the train rails were filled with water from a cylindrical container carried by the train. These were for sole use of people working for the railways station. We invited Zainab, begging her to tell us one of her folk's tales. She sat down with a faint smile narrating the story of 'Fatima the beautiful' and a couple more of exiting and fearful tales. The boy sitting on her lap, absorbed in the tales, got scared cuddled her and would not let her go.

Unlike the residence buildings, the railways station was built as a normal building with flat roof and spacious three rooms without a bath or WC. One room was used as an office, one as store for the railway equipments and the third was a large room left empty which was utilized by Sheik Mahmoud for the school. There was a single rail track. Two passenger trains per week passed through and halted for less than five minutes at the station and a couple of goods trains per week. The boys got very excited whenever a passenger train arrived . . . so many people crowded in and on top of the train wagons . . . they wished that they would be one of them and dreamt of their next holidays to take the train to Karema the end or terminal of the track to the north and from there they would take the slow steamer heading north to their village `Ombokol` on the western side of the Nile, a trip that took almost three days.

About five peoples were assigned to maintain the railway track. They had a trolley which was dragged every morning and placed on the train rails and hand driven by four people, two on each side facing each other. The trolley was first loaded with tools necessary to repair the rails if need arises. The boss or Hikimdar as he was called sat on the trolley in a position to allow him to inspect the tracks, while the trolley was driven along. It was a spectacular scene watching them swinging up and down along the rails and chatting till they disappeared into the horizon.

Books by the author:

- *Enduring the pain(Novel)*
- *Mirage(poetry)*
- *Episodes(Novel)*
- *Hermann Hesse writings I (in Arabic)*
- *Hermann Hesse writings II (in Arabic)*

- *Demography, Scientific terminology (Eng./Arabic)*
- *Terminology (CD)*
- *Mathematics for computers*
- *Scientific terminology,*
  (Math. & Stat. Eng. /Arabic)
- *Scientific terminology,*
  (Math. Stat. & demography
  Eng. /Arabic)

To order visit
http://www.exact-it.com/Books.html